BIONICLE®

BIONICLE®

FIND THE POWER,

LIVE THE LEGEND

The legend comes alive in these exciting BIONICLE® books:

BIONICLE Chronicles
#1 Tale of the Toa
#2 Beware the Bohrok
#3 Makuta's Revenge
#4 Tales of the Masks

BIONICLE: Mask of Light
The Official Guide to BIONICLE
BIONICLE Collector's Sticker Book
BIONICLE: Metru Nui: City of Legends
BIONICLE: Rahi Beasts
BIONICLE: Dark Hunters
BIONICLE: World

BIONICLE Adventures
#1 Mystery of Metru Nui
#2 Trial by Fire
#3 The Darkness Below
#4 Legends of Metru Nui
#5 Voyage of Fear
#6 Maze of Shadows
#7 Web of the Visorak
#8 Challenge of the Hordika
#9 Web of Shadows
#10 Time Trap

BIONICLE Legends
#1 Island of Doom
#2 Dark Destiny
#3 Power Play
#4 Legacy of Evil
#5 Inferno
#6 City of the Lost
#7 Prisioners of the Pit

BIONICLE®

Downfall

by Greg Farshtey

SCHOLASTIC INC.
New York Toronto London Auckland Sydney
Mexico City New Delhi Hong Kong Buenos Aires

ISBN-13: 978-0-439-89037-3
ISBN-10: 0-439-89037-3

12 11 10 9 8 7 6 5 4 3 2 1 8 9 10/0

Printed in the U.S:A.
First printing, January 2008

For Lena, with respect and gratitude

BIONICLE®

Downfall

INTRODUCTION

Toa Mahri Hahli sat on the shore of Metru Nui's silver sea and gazed sadly out at the water. She had always hoped to see this city again, and its people — but even in her worst nightmares, she had never expected to return with the tale she brought.

Kopeke, a Ko-Matoran, walked slowly up to her and sat down without saying a word. Once the residents of Metru Nui learned Hahli had become a Toa, it was necessary that one of their number be appointed to act as Chronicler in her place. The choice of the city elders had been Kopeke, long a trusted aide to Turaga Nuju. He adjusted his mask and then waited in silence for Hahli to begin to speak.

"I don't envy you," the Toa Mahri of Water said finally. "When Takua was Chronicler, he wrote of many victories and many defeats. One of the first events I had to record during my time in the post was the destruction of the village of Ta-Koro. But never did I think such a tragic history as this would ever need to be written. Still, Turaga Nokama says sometimes the best way to make sadness go away is to let it float from you on a tide of words."

Kopeke nodded, but said nothing. He was never the most social of Matoran, and this situation clearly made him uncomfortable. Still, the Turaga felt the so-often-silent Matoran was the best choice for the job of Chronicler — after all, it is impossible to learn anything while you are speaking.

Hahli took a deep breath. She knew it was getting close to the time to she would have to leave Ga-Metru and join her friends for the memorial in the Coliseum. But how she would make it through that ceremony, she had no idea.

"It happened . . . so fast," she said. "One moment, he was there in front of me . . . the next . . ."

She paused, the words hard to come by. Kopeke looked away, not sure what he should do in this situation. "You know, Jaller always used to say that Toa were invincible, because the things they stand for — unity, duty, and destiny — are invincible," Toa Hahli continued. "Oh, we had seen them injured, even defeated temporarily, but somehow they — *we* — always stood to fight again. Even in the worst moments, I thought surely we would win out and return home again. That's what Toa do, isn't it? That's what heroes do."

Kopeke didn't know how to respond. Even knowing that most Toa began their lives as Matoran, he had always thought of them as something different. They were better, stronger, more capable, and able to handle any problem. Seeing one so troubled and in so much pain shook him more than he wanted to admit. But he knew he had a job to do, an important job — to make sure no one ever forgot what had happened in the depths of the Pit.

"If you write *nothing* else, Chronicler, write this," said Hahli. "Sometimes a hero has to do something else besides beat the villains and come home covered in glory. Sometimes, he has to make a sacrifice so that a lot of people — people he's never even met, and who don't know his name — can live."

Kopeke scratched her words down on a stone tablet, and then waited expectantly. After a few more moments, Hahli began to speak again, her words transporting the Chronicler to the black waters beneath Mahri Nui and a time only a few days past. . . .

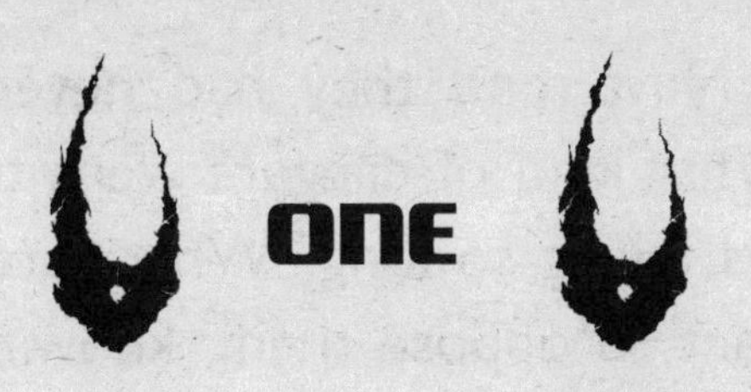

ONE

Three Days Ago . . .
Metru Nui

Turaga Nuju sat in his observatory high atop a Knowledge Tower in Ko-Metru. It was not a chamber he expected to be using for much longer. Its purpose was the study of the stars above Metru Nui, but there were precious few still burning. Those that remained were rapidly fading. When the last of them was extinguished, the universe would be on its final countdown to destruction.

More than anything, it was the feeling of helplessness that was driving him mad. The Toa Nuva had left some time ago to try to save the Great Spirit Mata Nui and the universe, but never returned. Jaller had led a team of Matoran to find the Toa Nuva, and they had never returned either. What kind of dangers were they facing? What was taking so long? What sort of lunatic would want to oppose them, knowing that the fate of all existence hinged on their success?

They must find the Mask of Life and use it to save Mata Nui, thought Nuju. *And they must find it soon or a sky full of dead stars will be the least of our worries.*

The depths of the Pit,
not far from Mahri Nui.

Hydraxon aimed his Cordak blaster at the Mask of Life and fired.

As jailer of the Pit, he knew it was his job to recapture any escaped inmates and prevent them from getting their hands on dangerous weapons. So when he stumbled on the brutish ex-prisoner named Nocturn carrying the Kanohi Ignika, he carried out his duty: He subdued the runner, seized the glowing mask, and prepared to destroy it. It would be better for all concerned if a mask this powerful was in pieces and couldn't be used by the wrong beings.

A mini-rocket from the blaster sped on its way to the mask. Then something strange happened — a powerful current slammed into the rocket, throwing it off course. It plowed into a nearby boulder and exploded, sending debris flying through the water.

Before the jailer could wonder about the freak current, another one hit him, hurling him far away from the Mask of Life. This time, he spotted the source. It was a Toa of Water leading an army of rays and flanked by one of the escaped Barraki prisoners — Mantax, if he recalled correctly.

"Back off!" shouted the Toa. "Keep away from that mask!"

Hydraxon's answer was to launch multiple rockets, and then dive for cover as the explosions went off. As he hoped, the blasts stunned the Toa, Mantax, and Nocturn. He vaulted out from behind a rock and went for the mask. His hand was almost upon it when a claw slashed down and pinned his wrist to the ocean floor. It belonged to the Toa, who was reaching for the mask herself. Hydraxon aimed his blaster at it again, but she managed to knock it aside. The explosive charge hit in front of the Kanohi Ignika, sending it spiraling through the water —

And right into the claws of Mantax.

Toa Hahli and Hydraxon, their fight forgotten, moved as one after the Barraki. But as soon as they came within a hundred yards, weakness seized them. At 50 yards, they were too tired to keep swimming and sank to the bottom. Mantax, on the other hand, looked stronger than ever.

"The Mask of Life is mine now," the Barraki hissed. "And it will stay mine. Tell Pridak and the others to meet me at the Razor Whale's Teeth in one day — unarmed, no armies — where I will dictate my terms. Any tricks and the mask will be destroyed."

"I don't make deals with runners," snarled Hydraxon. "You want to shatter that headgear? Go right ahead."

"Shut up!" Hahli whispered harshly to the jailer. "I need that mask — the universe *needs* it — try anything, and I will personally show you the meaning of 'dead in the water.'"

Surrounded by his rays, Mantax swam off with the mask. As soon as he was gone, Hahli and Hydraxon felt their strength returning. The jailer immediately turned to look for Nocturn, only to find that his prisoner was gone. He whirled around and glared at Hahli.

"Now see what your interference has caused!" Hydraxon said. "A few seconds more and that mask would have been dust. Instead, it's in the hands of a Barraki."

"A few seconds more and we all would have been dust," Hahli replied. "And who in blazes are you, anyway?"

Hydraxon started to snap off the obvious answer that he was himself, an Order of Mata Nui member, jailer of the Pit, but something stopped him. Flashes of memory kept intruding of a life that couldn't have been his — a life as a Po-Matoran in an undersea city. He saw this

Matoran, whose name was Dekar, swimming through night-dark waters and battling sea creatures who threatened his home. But what did any of this matter to Hydraxon? This had no connection to his past or identity . . . did it?

"Who I am is my business," he said finally. "Staying out of my way is yours."

By the time the other Toa Mahri tracked her down, Hahli was alone. Hydraxon had departed, despite her efforts to talk him out of it. An attempt to make him stay by force had also failed, but a little more painfully.

She was a little surprised to see the robotic Maxilos, former guard of the Pit, and his pet Spinax sticking so close to Toa Matoro. But there would be time to question her comrade later about his choice of traveling companions. For now, she gave Jaller and the rest a rapid briefing on Mantax and the Mask of Life.

"And I have no doubt Hydraxon is going after him, even if he did swim off in the opposite direction," Hahli finished.

"Someone needs to follow him," said Jaller, "while the rest of us make sure Mantax gets his wish for a meeting."

"Let's send Maxilos," suggested Matoro. "Spinax here is supposed to be able to track a protodite across a planet, so finding one well-armed lunatic shouldn't be a problem. And I'm sure Maxilos would be happy to help out... wouldn't you, robot?"

Inside, Matoro was smiling. He knew what none of the others did: that the shell of Maxilos was inhabited by the spirit of the evil Makuta. He also knew Makuta didn't want the other Toa Mahri to have that knowledge. That left "Maxilos" no choice but to go along with the Toa of Ice's suggestion.

Without a word, the crimson robot turned and left, followed closely by Spinax. Matoro couldn't help but feel relieved to watch him go.

"This is our chance to get the mask away from the Barraki," said Toa Hewkii. "But it won't be easy... or pretty. Things are bad enough down here now, but once we have the mask...

well, the Barraki won't stop at anything to get it back."

"A lot of innocents could get hurt," Hahli agreed.

"Then let's see that they are ever-safe," Kongu offered. "Who volunteers to deep-talk with Defilak?"

"First we make sure the trap is set," said Jaller. "And then we'll all talk to him. Maybe by then we can figure out how to tell a proud Matoran he has to run."

Under stone markers of truce, the Toa Mahri were able to pass word to the Barraki about Mantax's request. Only Ehlek refused to let a Toa approach, but he had already received the news from Nocturn. The reactions among the former allies ranged from intrigued — what price would Mantax want for the mask? — to annoyed and all the way up to murderous rage.

Grimly, they made their preparations. Armies were ordered to stay well away from the meeting site and weapons laid aside, at least the obvious ones. If each of them made sure a dagger or two was safely hidden somewhere near the Razor Whale's Teeth, well, that was just Barraki being cautious, at least in most cases. But one of them had made up his mind to actually use the blades, Mask of Life at stake or not.

Mantax was busy getting ready for this meeting as well. He was not particularly fearful for his safety, for he had already deduced how the Mask of Life had "cursed" him. He had become a true parasite, draining the life energy from anyone or anything that came too close to him. It seemed to work in much the same way as the attacks of Kalmah's squid, only Mantax did not have to be in physical contact as they did to grow stronger. Unfortunately, for the power to work, he had to be holding on to the mask. That meant leaving it behind, safely hidden, was no longer an option.

It didn't matter. Once he showed the others the other little item he would be bringing with him, they would lose all interest in attacking him. They would be too busy tearing each other apart, and once they were done, Mantax would be the only one left standing.

Defilak had said nothing for a long time, and simply listened as the Toa Mahri explained. His memories of life before living underwater were fragmentary at best, as were those of the other Mahri Nui Matoran. To discover that there was an island far above on the surface of the sea that had once been their home was overwhelming.

"When Voya Nui broke off its continent and shot to the surface, you were there," said Matoro. "You and your fellow Matoran. Over time, new land formed around the island, and Mahri Nui was built on that land. But the ground was unstable — it broke off and Mahri Nui sank down here. Until a few days ago, everyone on Voya Nui assumed you were all dead."

"I said when we met there were friends who would want to meet you," said Hahli softly. "They will welcome you back with joy."

"Back?" asked Defilak. "How would we go back?"

"The cord," said Jaller, pointing to the long stone "chain" that linked Mahri Nui to Voya Nui. "We came down it to get here — now you and your people will travel up to safety. It's the only way."

Defilak shook his head. "Even if what you say is true, we cannot fear-flee from our home. We cannot let the Barraki win."

"They aren't going to win," Matoro replied. "It may be that *no one* is going to win. Maybe all anyone can hope for is to survive, and this is your best chance at that. Your sacrifice is needless, Defilak — fighting and dying is what we are here to do. Your job is to live and help your people to do the same."

Defilak looked around at his city, his people manning the defenses, and the black water that surrounded Mahri Nui. He remembered the struggle to build an existence down here, all the triumphs and all the tragedies. He did not remember this Voya Nui or the Matoran the Toa insisted would be waiting above, but there was one thing the heroes were saying that he knew to be true:

No Matoran belonged down here. This was not their world.

"What do we have to do?" he said finally.

As swiftly as possible, the Toa assembled all of the Mahri Nui Matoran and led them to the base of the cord. The maze of stone tunnels that connected the village to the island above had been heavily damaged by a monstrous Rahi's attack, resulting in virtually the entire cord being flooded. With the six Toa in the lead, the strange procession entered an outer tunnel and began the long journey to the surface.

The heroes were watchful and wary. They had almost died on the journey down to Mahri Nui at the hands of a group calling themselves Zyglak. If they attacked again, scores of Matoran lives might be lost before they could be driven back.

Strangely, though, there was no sign of them. In a way, that was more disturbing than another battle would have been. If they were here, why were they hiding? And if they had fled, where had they gone — Voya Nui? Were the Toa Mahri leading the Matoran right into a trap?

It was Hahli who found part of the answer. Swimming ahead, her fins brushed against something floating up near the roof of the tunnel. She glanced up, saw a Zyglak, and instinctively aimed her Cordak blaster. But there was no need — the Zyglak was dead. So were all the others she ran across as she moved on, until the cord resembled a watery graveyard.

Hahli turned back to report to the others. Then something shot out of a side tunnel and slammed into her. At first, she thought the long, narrow form belonged to a sea snake of some kind. Then it wrapped around her and its face loomed out of the darkness . . . a horribly familiar face.

"Hakann!" she cried.

The crimson Piraka snarled and began to constrict, trying to squeeze the Toa to death. Hahli hurled herself at the tunnel wall, slamming her serpentine attacker against the stone. Stunned, Hakann loosened his grip and slipped away.

Hahli couldn't believe her eyes as she looked at her old enemy. The Piraka's body was gone. He was now just a long spine with a head attached, moving through the water like a hideous eel. Hakann closed in again, but Hahli slashed at him with her talons and drove him back.

"What happened to you?" she asked.

"We were racing to get the Mask of Life, and thanks to Vezok, wound up down in a pool of water," Hakann hissed. "It . . . changed us . . . into freaks. We . . . slithered . . . down this cord before Axonn or the Voya Nui Matoran could stop us. And when these reptiles tried to get in our way . . ."

"You killed them," Hahli finished. "Where are your friends, Piraka?"

"Right now?" Hakann asked, with a smile. "Attacking yours."

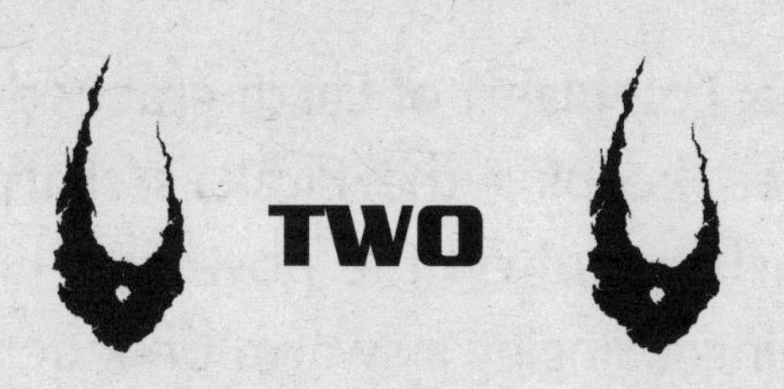

TWO

The cord was chaos.

The five Piraka snakes had struck from both sides at the rear of the procession, tearing through the ranks of the Matoran. Jaller's Mask of Sonar had given him a moment's warning, long enough to ensure there were Toa ready to fight off the assault. But even they were stunned by the identity of their enemies.

"Didn't we already beat these guys?" Hewkii asked as he whipped his chain around Vezok and slammed him onto the ground.

"Not well enough, I guess," Kongu answered, dodging a laser blast from Zaktan. "Or else they're just stubborn."

"Your fault!" screamed Avak, his snake-like form encircling Nuparu's arm. "If you had just let us have the Mask of Life, this would never have happened!"

The Toa Mahri of Earth grabbed his foe by the throat, keeping the Piraka's sharp teeth at bay. Kongu called on the power of his Mask of Summoning, bringing a swarm of undersea insect life out of the walls of the cord. The tiny creatures affixed themselves to the Piraka's spines, stinging them again and again.

"What's the point of this, Zaktan?" Jaller asked, trying in vain to hit the Piraka with flame bursts. "You want the Mask of Life, and we don't have it. Fighting us accomplishes nothing."

Zaktan coiled the end of his spine around a Matoran's throat and began to squeeze. "Wrong. It brings you pain. And we want to go on bringing you pain, Toa. Now lay down your weapons and surrender, or this Matoran dies — along with many more. You know how many we can kill before you can stop us."

Jaller's eyes met those of Zaktan's captive, a Ga-Matoran named Idris. There was a question in her gaze. The Toa nodded, and a split second later, Idris triggered her electro-blade and thrust it up toward Zaktan. There was a bright flash and the Piraka screamed, uncoiling at the same time. Idris leapt to the side as Jaller's flames brought molten rock raining down on the Piraka leader.

Suddenly, the Toa Mahri were cut off from the Matoran. Walls had appeared on either end of the tunnel, boxing them in, and the water was being rapidly drained out of this new chamber. No longer able to breathe air, the Toa's senses began to swim in the now dry environment. On the other side of the wall, Avak smiled. His power to create the perfect prison for any enemy was still intact, even if his body was not.

"Fish out of water," he chuckled. "Gasp for breath in your last moments, Toa, but don't worry — we'll take care of your Matoran friends once you're gone."

Jaller heard a loud humming in his ears. He guessed it was one more sign of approaching death from suffocation. Instead, it was the herald of a powerful jolt of electricity that shot through the tunnel, shocking Toa, Piraka, and Matoran into unconsciousness.

* * *

The Toa Mahri of Fire awoke with a start. He was lying facedown in a pool of water. Below him, he could see the other Toa Mahri reviving, but no sign of the Piraka or the Matoran.

Flipping over, he peered up through the water. He now realized he was near the top of the cord, almost to the point where it emerged on Voya Nui. Crouching near the water's edge was Axonn, the last remaining guardian of that island. Beyond him, Jaller could see the Matoran of Voya Nui embracing their brothers and sisters from Mahri Nui.

"You and the Piraka took the brunt of the blast," said Axonn. "I am glad to see you survived."

"Me, too," said Jaller. "Where are the Piraka?"

"They have been . . . taken care of," said Axonn, his tone making it clear he had no intention of explaining further. "You have been through a war, I see."

Jaller glanced down. His armor was damaged, as were his weapons, the result of ongoing battles with the Barraki and their armies. "And it's still going on," he replied.

Matoro swam up beside Jaller. "Meaning it's time for you to stop being so mysterious, Axonn. I was told by . . . someone . . . that we have to shatter the cord linking Mahri Nui and Voya Nui to complete our mission, and that will result in the destruction of both islands. Is that true?"

Axonn nodded. "It is and it is not. You must destroy the cord, yes, for it holds Voya Nui here. And yes, Mahri Nui will be destroyed. But Voya Nui will return to its home and you must go with it. That is where the Mask of Life must be used if the universe is to survive."

"All right, then we use the Cordak blasters and blow it now," said Jaller.

"No!" Axonn answered. "You must not! First, you must have the Mask of Life in your hands — for once the cord is shattered, you will have no time to retrieve it. And second, you must give me time to get the Matoran to safety. There are chambers underground where they can stay until Voya Nui is back where it belongs. The alternative is they will be swept away by the incredible forces you are about to unleash."

Matoro reached up and clasped Axonn's hand. "You do what you have to do, then," said the Toa of Ice. "We will get the mask. I promise you that."

Jaller glanced at Matoro, wondering just who this grim, determined Toa was — it certainly was not the Matoro he had set out from Metru Nui with, so many days ago.

"Time is of the essence," said Axonn. "Follow me."

The guardian took a deep breath, dove into the flooded cord and began to swim. The Toa Mahri followed. Not far down, Axonn turned into a side chamber. He paused, treaded water, and pointed.

Inside the chamber was a monstrous, insectoid Rahi. Its head turned slowly to observe the newcomers even as its multiple legs swayed in the current in what looked like a bizarre dance. Even stranger was that the beast was outfitted with mechanical add-ons and weaponry, making it look more like a living vehicle than a creature. A large chain around its midsection kept it from leaving the chamber.

Hahli looked at Axonn with an expression of distaste on her features. As a Toa of Water, it disturbed her to see a Rahi confined or altered in this way. Axonn ignored her. Instead, he aimed his ax at the wall and fired a blast of energy. When he was done, a message had been carved into the stone: "Get in."

With varying degrees of reluctance, the Toa Mahri climbed through the creature's armor plating and crowded into the inside of the Rahi. Hewkii immediately made for the exit, not at all liking being confined inside a living thing. Jaller put a restraining hand on him and gestured for the Toa of Stone to relax.

Outside, Axonn swung his ax and shattered the chain that held the Rahi in place. The creature immediately began to move, drawing its legs in and darting out of the chamber entrance. It made instinctively for its home, the waters around Mahri Nui, twisting and turning through the winding tunnels of the cord.

Before the Toa Mahri could even grow used to the abrupt changes in direction, small techno-organic appendages sprang out of the walls and seized them. The "hands" pulled at their armor, stripping it off them, then grabbed their masks and weapons as well. It happened so quickly the Toa couldn't prevent the theft, and by the time they acted, their property had been pulled into the walls of the creature's body. An instant later, the items were back, but with a difference: All the battle damage had been repaired.

Hewkii examined his armor and weapons closely, then shook his head. "A few more of these Rahi and all of Ta-Metru would be out of work."

"Let's worry about our own jobs," said Hahli, adjusting her mask. "We still have a mask to get and a cord to shatter."

"If someone doesn't beat us to it," Matoro said, thinking of Maxilos, Hydraxon, and the six Barraki.

The Toa of Ice had never been much interested in competitive sports like kolhii, or in wagering on the outcome (something that was frowned on by the Turaga anyway). Nor did he like hypothetical questions like "If Tahu and Kopaka fought, who would win?" He knew there were always variables, unpredictable circumstances that could affect the outcome of a contest. Victory did not always go to the strongest or to the righteous or to those who deserved to win — if it did, Makuta would have been ashes long ago. He would never have gambled on the outcome of the Toa Mahri's mission, either. But in this case, it wasn't because logic said there was no way to predict the result, or because he felt wagering was wrong.

He just didn't like the odds.

One of those unpredictable circumstances was waiting down below. For most of its life, the creature called Gadunka had been a tiny, inoffensive bottom-dweller. Although gifted with row upon row of sharp teeth, it was too small to be any real threat to anything bigger than an inch or so. Of course, that was before it took refuge under what it thought was a strangely glowing rock and began to change.

That "rock" was the Mask of Life. A minute portion of its power rapidly changed Gadunka from an inoffensive meal for bigger fish to a monstrosity with a mouth big enough to swallow a Takea shark whole.

However, its intelligence had not grown along with its body. Gadunka was still governed by the same drives it had always been: eat and survive. Now it was simply much better at doing both. Being a territorial creature by nature, it was used to ruling a fragment of a reef or a bit of rock, fighting off all competition for that space. In its new form, it saw potential for claiming a domain a great deal bigger for itself.

There was, as always, a problem. Other beings were within the bounds of the area it wanted for itself. It could see six of them, all obvious predators, but none as big or as dangerous as Gadunka knew itself to be. They would be easy to get rid of.

Gadunka's eyes narrowed. One of the six was carrying the glowing rock. That wasn't right. The rock belonged to Gadunka. When they were driven off, that would be left behind, it decided.

The creature opened its cavernous mouth and bellowed, the noise scattering prey fish for hundreds of yards around. Gadunka had power, and now it had purpose as well. It began the long swim toward its six targets, eager for the thrill of battle.

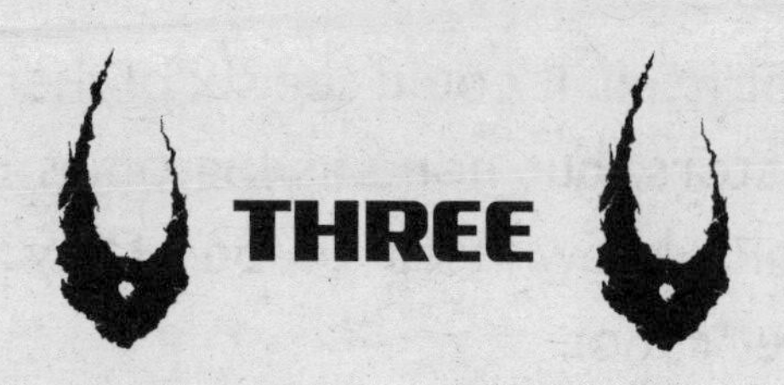

THREE

Maxilos and Spinax caught up with Hydraxon on an undersea mountain overlooking the Barraki's meeting place. He had made an effort not to follow too closely, so that Hydraxon would not hear his approach. His caution was wasted when Gadunka's bellow ripped through the water, startling Hydraxon. The jailer turned then, seeking the source. He spotted the crimson robot closing in and visibly relaxed.

"I wondered where you had disappeared to," said Hydraxon. "Come on, we have a runner to catch."

Maxilos's face remained cold and still, but inside, the mind of Makuta was amused. Hydraxon still believed Maxilos was nothing more than his loyal robot prison guard. He had no idea there was a ghost in the machine.

Under ordinary circumstances, Makuta would have gladly joined in any effort to hunt down and destroy the Barraki. The warlords were upstarts with delusions of godhood, too bitter to be trusted and too independent to be used. They would have to be eliminated at some point, he had no doubt. But not, he reminded himself, while the Kanohi Ignika was in their possession. Mata Nui needed that mask to live, and the Great Spirit had to live if Makuta was to someday rule.

"Turn back," he said, in the flat, robotic voice of Maxilos. "There are two dozen escaped prisoners two kio to the east of our position that must be recaptured."

Hydraxon frowned. "Two dozen? That will make for a busy day. But none of them have a glowing Mask of Power, I'll bet, and this runner does. Keep an eye on that mob and I will join you when I've caught my prey."

Well, I tried, thought Makuta. *I wanted to do this the easy way, but if he insists on being destroyed, who am I to say no?*

Maxilos raised its arm and a bolt of electricity shot from it, striking Hydraxon square in the chest. This was followed by a wave of magnetism that dragged the jailer down to the sea bottom by his armor and pinned him to the ground. Then came a burst of sonics, sufficient to turn a normal being's mind to mush. For someone with Hydraxon's enhanced senses, it was sheer agony.

"I asked you nicely to turn back," said Maxilos, although the words were Makuta's. "I never ask twice."

"You're . . . not . . . Maxilos . . ." Hydraxon gasped through the pain.

Maxilos reached out and touched the jailer's mind, scanning it. Then the robot gave a short, sharp laugh. "And you're not Hydraxon . . . you only think you are. The real Hydraxon is dead, slain by Takadox and buried in the rubble of the original Pit. You're a copy, just some wandering Matoran the Mask of Life decided to have some sport with. You're not even worth the time it's taking to demolish you."

For an instant, the expression of suffering left Hydraxon's face, to be replaced by one of rage. With enormous effort, he forced two words from his mouth: "Manas zya!"

Even as Spinax suddenly wheeled and launched itself at Maxilos's throat, the mind of Makuta was analyzing. "Manas" was the Matoran word for "monster," but "zya" . . . that was an ancient term, so old even Makuta barely recalled it. Judging from Spinax's reaction, its meaning was pretty clear.

Spinax was clawing and snapping at Maxilos's armor and doing damage. Maxilos swept the beast away, but it kept coming back to the attack. The distraction had given Hydraxon a chance to recover and the jailer was back on his feet, already unlimbering a dagger.

"Spinax worked with Maxilos, but he *belongs* to me," said Hydraxon. "He won't stop attacking until you're down for good. And don't bother running — there's nowhere he can't find you."

"Run?" snarled Maxilos, as he flung Spinax away. "A Makuta does not run! Away from me, you miserable creature!"

Hydraxon had never met a member of the Brotherhood of Makuta before. But his memories contained enough overheard conversations from Pit prisoners to have some idea of the level of power he was dealing with. He would have to strike without mercy.

Twin daggers flew, burying themselves in the joints of Maxilos's left arm and left leg. Hydraxon knew every detail of the robot's construction, and just where to hit it. Both limbs went dead.

Maxilos opened its mouth and screamed, but not in pain. Instead, it was an attack. The sound smashed Hydraxon down and again ravaged his mind. Maxilos advanced, maintaining the power scream and tearing the daggers out of its metallic body as it walked. The jailer fired his Cordak blaster, shattering part of an undersea mountain and bringing a rain of boulders down on Maxilos. The scream was cut off as the avalanche buried the robot.

* * *

At the appointed hour, the Barraki had all assembled at the rock formation called the Razor Whale's Teeth. As requested, they had come without the support of their undersea armies, though no one was foolish enough to believe the legions were far off. Kalmah was the first to arrive, taking the opportunity to scout the area for possible sites of ambush. Ehlek straggled in last and stayed far away from the others.

For most of their lives, these six warlords had been allies, if not necessarily the best of friends. There had been arguments over the millennia, threats, even physical conflict — but never had they actually gone to war against each other. That had all changed in the last day. A combination of accident, their own bad tempers, and a little "help" from the Toa had fractured the six into four factions — Pridak and Takadox, Kalmah and Carapar, while Ehlek and Mantax stood alone.

The object of their dispute was the Mask of Life. They believed that the mask would be able to reverse the mutation sparked by the waters around them, which left them water-breathing monstrosities. Once they were back to what they had been — air-breathing peaks of physical perfection — they intended to reclaim their lost kingdoms on the land and begin anew their march to power.

Of course, if only one of the Barraki were to be aided by the Mask of Life, he and he alone would be in a position to conquer. The now defunct League of Six Kingdoms would be reborn, but as one kingdom under one warlord.

If the Barraki had known the facts about the Kanohi Ignika, not just the legend, then they would have been assured the mask could do what they hoped. Whether it could be made to do so was another matter. If it did, though, its effects need not be limited to just the being who possessed the mask, so all six could benefit. But for beings who had spent their lives seizing and defending territory, sharing did not come naturally. After 80,000 years of confinement in the

Pit, the Barraki could be forgiven if every minor slight became a major offense and mutual suspicion flared into open war.

But some things, Mantax knows, cannot be forgiven . . . ever.

"You all came," he began, climbing up on a rock. His five former allies watched, a mixture of anger, uneasiness, and greed on their faces. "Of course you did. You want what I have. But then, that's nothing new. When we lived on land, you coveted my kingdom and my power. Under the sea, you desired to know my secrets. Well, now you will."

Mantax crouched down, never taking his eyes off the others. He picked up a small, triangular shaped stone from the top of the boulder and held it close to his chest. If any of his visitors were reacting to the sight of the object, they were hiding it well.

"Ever since we escaped from the Pit 1,000 years ago, I have been returning there," Mantax continued. "You all wondered why. Takadox and

Kalmah even followed me there, trying to learn my reason. Now I can tell you: I was searching for something . . . and I have found it."

Mantax held up the stone so the other Barraki could see it. One side of the rock was blank, but the other had the symbol of the Brotherhood of Makuta carved upon it. Every Barraki knew that symbol well, for it had been an army of the Brotherhood that had defeated them in battle so long ago. That defeat had resulted in their exile to the Pit.

"Do you know what this is?" Mantax said quietly. "One of you does, I know. It's a Brotherhood tablet of transit. In an era long past, whoever held this could not be detained by the Brotherhood for any reason. It was a sign to Makuta the universe over that the bearer was a valued ally of that 'honorable' organization."

"We know all that! Get to the point, Mantax," snarled Pridak. Then he smiled, revealing row upon row of sharp teeth. "Or else I will get to mine, and mine are infinitely sharper."

"I found this down in the rubble of our old cells," Mantax answered, his tone as cold as the black water around them. "It belonged to one of us. There was only one reason a Barraki would have this and hold on to it so long."

He paused for a long moment to let his words sink in. Sensing Mantax intended to make a dramatic pronouncement, Kalmah decided to deprive him of the satisfaction. "He thought he might need it. And the only reason for that —"

"— Would be if he knew the Brotherhood was going to come after us!" said Carapar, his glance darting to each of his fellows in turn. "Someone double-crossed us!"

Pridak's mouth was set in a grim line. "Now it all makes sense. 80,000 years ago, one of our number informed the Brotherhood that we planned a revolt against the Great Spirit Mata Nui. In return for that betrayal, he was given that tablet. Once we were defeated, it would have allowed him to walk away while the rest of us were executed."

"But things changed," said Ehlek. "The Brotherhood captured us, true, but then that other creature — that Botar — appeared from nowhere and sent us to the Pit. Even Makuta didn't seem to know who he was."

"All right, but then why keep the tablet?" asked Takadox. "What good would it do down here?"

"Insurance," said Kalmah, "against the hoped-for day when we escape. If the Brotherhood is still active, they will be after us the second we reappear on land — after all of us, that is, except one . . . the one with that tablet."

"You want to share in the power of the Mask of Life," snapped Mantax. "I want the traitor. One of you will confess now, and face punishment — or none of you will ever see this mask again!"

The six Barraki glared at each other in uncomfortable silence. No one spoke. Pridak took a step toward Mantax, who pulled back, holding the mask high as if he would smash it on the rocks. A scaly hand reached for a hidden dagger.

A faraway rumble became a roar. The Barraki looked up as one to see an avalanche heading right for them. The six scattered as boulders rained down around them. Mantax darted away, mask in one hand, tablet in the other. A dagger flew by, slashing the organic tissue in his left arm. He dropped the mask to the sandy ocean bottom.

"You won't be needing that," his attacker said, poison in his voice. The shadowy figure reached out and twisted Mantax's arm until he dropped the tablet. "Or that."

Mantax whirled in the water to find a dagger at his throat. "You! Of course, it had to be — who else would —"

"You know, I really didn't intend to end your life, you miserable mud-dweller," said Takadox. "But I must admit, I will enjoy the peace and quiet when you're gone."

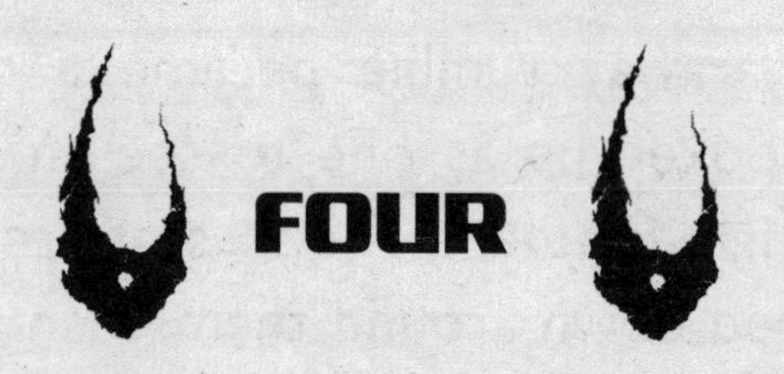

FOUR

The Toa Mahri spilled out of their living transport just as the avalanche struck the Barraki. They saw the six villains take off in different directions. Matoro and Jaller immediately spotted the mask in Mantax's possession and Takadox following. It was only when Hahli cried out that anyone noticed the monstrous sea Rahi who was in pursuit of Takadox.

"I guess we split up," said Nuparu.

"Jaller and I will go after the mask," said Matoro.

"Nuparu and I will keep the other Barraki out of trouble," offered Hahli.

"That leaves gruesome for me," said Hewkii, smiling. "Now I can't say you never gave me anything."

"Enough!" snapped Jaller. "Less talking, more hitting."

* * *

Hewkii already knew the quickest way to beat the monstrous Rahi called Gadunka. A simple application of the power of the Mask of Gravity would leave the creature as mobile as the average rock, if not as decorative. But somehow it didn't feel right. Hewkii was an athlete, he lived for competition. Where was the sport in winning a battle only because he had a Mask of Power and Gadunka didn't?

"All right, so I'll try it without the mask," he said to himself. "But if it looks like it's him or me . . ."

The Rahi didn't know about Hewkii's decision and didn't care. It lunged, jaws snapping, and the Toa of Stone barely evaded in time. The second attack was faster, and this time Gadunka caught Hewkii's leg in his mouth. The Rahi shook his head violently from side to side, threatening to snap the Toa in two.

I can play by those rules too, thought Hewkii. He reached out, grabbed a rock wall, and then used his leverage to kick forward and send Gadunka into the hard stone. The impact made the Rahi release him. Hewkii landed unsteadily on the sea floor in time to see Gadunka charging again.

The Rahi opened its massive jaws. Too late to dodge, Hewkii instead thrust his warblade into the creature's mouth, using the weapon to keep the beast's jaws propped open. The Toa then reared back and struck with all his might, sending Gadunka flying.

By the time Hewkii reached the spot where the Rahi had landed, it had already spat out the warblade. Hewkii used his elemental power to form fists of stone to batter Gadunka. As fast as he created them, the Rahi bit them in two.

"You should really do something about that overbite," said Hewkii.

Gadunka lunged forward and head-butted the Toa in the abdomen. When Hewkii doubled over, the Rahi struck him hard on the head with his pincer. Hewkii went down and Gadunka stomped on his back with its clawed foot until the Toa stopped moving.

Satisfied the battle was over, Gadunka gave

a roar of victory and started to swim away. The next instant, a chain wrapped itself around the Rahi's midsection. Gadunka twisted itself around to bite through it, but just as its jaws closed on the metal, an electrical surge shot through the chain. The Rahi's body was wracked by spasms as thousands of volts shot through its frame.

"Don't turn your back on me," said Hewkii, holding on to the other end of the chain. "Bad enough you're a rampaging sea monster, at least be a polite one."

The shock and pain enraged Gadunka. It somehow managed to finish closing its jaws, its huge teeth snapping the chain. The Rahi staggered forward a few steps, then collapsed.

Hewkii took a few tentative steps forward to examine his foe. The creature was down, but still breathing. As the Toa bent to pick up the broken pieces of his chain, a heavy-lidded eye suddenly snapped open. Gadunka rolled, smashing into Hewkii and knocking the Toa off his feet. The Rahi snapped its pincer around the Toa's throat and began to squeeze.

* * *

Hahli and Nuparu saw the battle from far off and raced to their friend's aid. They had spent the last few minutes harassing four of the Barraki, but with limited success. The warlords were gathering their armies and it would only be a matter of minutes before they would be after the Mask of Life.

Nuparu dove, using his aqua blaster blade to send shockwaves through the water. Gadunka snarled but didn't loosen his grip on Hewkii. Distracted by the Toa of Earth, though, it never saw Hahli coming from the other direction. She rammed the Rahi hard enough to make him let go of the Toa of Stone. When it tried to return to the attack, she slashed the water with her talons to give it second thoughts.

"Are you all right?" she asked Hewkii.

"Thanks to you," said the Toa of Stone.

"Why didn't you use your mask power?" asked Hahli. "No, don't tell me, I can guess. This isn't the time for a contest of strength, brother — save it for when we're back home safe."

Not waiting for a response, Hahli used her control over water to create an underwater tidal wave. It hit Gadunka with devastating force, dropping the Rahi in his tracks.

This time, the Rahi wasn't getting back up. The three Toa Mahri swam in silence for the city of Mahri Nui and the final moments of their mission.

Matoro and Jaller made it to the ocean floor just as Takadox was about to strike. Matoro unleashed a blast of ice, freezing both dagger and hand. Takadox howled in pain. Mantax scrambled to his feet and head-butted his fellow Barraki, driving his head spikes into Takadox's abdomen. The paralyzing venom on the spikes immediately went to work.

"You . . . fool," muttered Takadox. "Do you think Toa will let you keep the mask? You've doomed . . . all of us . . ."

Mantax was startled by the explosion of a Cordah blaster rocket, launched from the back of Jaller's Hahnah crab. When he turned, Jaller dove, slamming into the Barraki. Mantax slashed the water with his pincers, but Jaller deflected the blow with his sword. The Barraki went for the mask, but Jaller was too fast for him. Using his control over heat and flame, he turned the water around his foe into a seething cauldron.

"Give it up," warned Jaller, "or some lucky Rahi is going to be feeding on boiled Barraki tonight."

Maxilos got to his feet. The avalanche had carried him all the way down to the Razor Whale's Teeth. His metallic body was badly damaged but still functional. There was no pain, for this robot frame couldn't feel any physical sensation. But there was anger. Hydraxon, he decided, would pay in full for his interference before this was all over.

He spotted a figure half walking, half dragging itself toward him. It was Takadox, his body struggling to fight off the paralyzing effects of Mantax's head spikes. He was losing the battle, but determined to still win the war. Approaching Maxilos, Takadox triggered his hypnotic power.

"You must . . . do as I say . . ." he whispered. "Find Mantax . . . kill Mantax . . . get the Mask of Life and . . ."

Maxilos backhanded Takadox, sending the Barraki flying. "Save your petty talents for the fish and the worms, Takadox," he growled. "And stop annoying your betters. You were pathetic as a warlord . . . more so as a traitor . . . and now this . . . oh, this is just laughable."

"If you think that's funny, you'll love this," said Matoro, hovering above. Not giving Maxilos any chance to react, he encased the robotic figure in ice that was beyond cold. The sudden, intense drop in temperature caused cracks to form in Maxilos's crimson armor. Tiny, barely visible wisps of greenish vapor began to drift through the cracks, only to freeze the instant they did.

"It ends here," said Matoro, as he continued to pour on the elemental energy. "One thousand years of fear and violence and darkness even in the day . . . it's time to stop it."

Matoro expected to hear Makuta's voice in his mind, threatening, pleading, cajoling, offering empty promises in return for freedom. But as the cold seeped into Makuta's armor and began to freeze even the energy inside, the words that sprang from mind to mind were worse than anything Matoro could have imagined.

I'm . . . proud . . . of you, said the mental voice of Makuta.

Mantax was down and Takadox was nowhere to be seen. Jaller had a free and clear shot at the Mask of Life, lying half-buried in the sand. Maybe Jaller had not contributed as much to the battle in the Pit as he would have liked, but he would have the honor of obtaining the mask.

Jaller went for the Kanohi Ignika. An armored hand grabbed his from behind, closing on his throat and cutting off his air. The next second, Jaller was being hauled off his feet by a battered Hydraxon.

"I think that mask belongs to me," said the Pit jailer. As casually as if he were throwing out rubbish, he hurled Jaller against a rock. The impact hurt, but Jaller wasn't about to let that stop him. Summoning all his willpower, he created a wall of flame several yards high and wide cutting Hydraxon off from the mask.

"Stupid runner," Hydraxon said. "I'll just go over or around it."

"No," said Jaller, shaking his head, "you won't."

The Toa of Fire's sonar had spotted what Hydraxon had not: Spinax, coming on the run, leaping to the attack. The hound went for Hydraxon's throat and it was all the jailer could do to keep the beast at bay.

Once again, Jaller moved to grab the Mask of Life. Once again, someone stopped him. This time, it was Maxilos, armor badly cracked and still half-covered in ice. "My thanks, Toa, for the well-timed wall of fire," said Makuta in the voice of the robot. "Not that I couldn't have freed myself, but I was curious to see just how far Matoro was willing to go. And by the way, Hydraxon, the hound may 'belong' to you, but I can be very . . . persuasive."

Maxilos advanced toward the Mask of Life. "Now I'll take that mask. You might drop it."

Jaller didn't know just what was going on. But his Mask of Sonar told him Matoro was approaching fast from above. This might be their best chance to get the mask, and the Toa of Fire wasn't going to blow it. He dove, slapping at the mask and sending it spiraling up through the water. "Matoro!" he yelled. "Grab it!"

The Toa of Ice reached out his hand, straining, and then the Mask of Life was in his grasp! He had it!

Matoro instantly braced himself, expecting an attack from Maxilos. But to his surprise, the possessed robot just stood there and watched. He didn't even make a move as Jaller swam to join his fellow Toa.

"What's the story with tall, red and spooky?" asked Jaller.

"More than time I told you," Matoro replied. "Let's talk as we travel — we have a cord to blow up."

FIVE

Maxilos watched Jaller and Matoro swim away with the mask. Hydraxon had finally succeeded in ripping Spinax loose from him. Maxilos felled the jailer with a well-placed blow before he could harm the hound. After all, there was no reason to harm a dumb Rahi. Not when harming intelligent beings was so much more fun.

He could imagine the questions that were running through the Toa's minds right now, especially Matoro's. Why would Makuta, master of shadows, sworn enemy of Toa, allow two to escape with the ultimate prize — the Mask of Life? Was he afraid? Weakened? Or did he have some plan to steal it back later?

None of the above, thought Maxilos. *Oh, I made a show of wanting the mask for myself... enlisting those foolish Piraka, as if those buffoons had a chance against even a team of novice Toa.*

True, they were lucky with the Toa Nuva, and I admit their alliance with Brutaka was a surprise — they came close to getting the mask. But I would have found a way to delay them, if need be.

Maxilos reached out and absently stroked Spinax's head. The hound was still in the thrall of Makuta's power to control animals. *Toa are honest and straightforward as a rule. That makes them one-dimensional and completely unprepared to deal with a complex entity such as myself.*

He reflected on his time in the Pit. When he had first encountered Matoro while wearing the shell of Maxilos, he had told the Toa of Ice, "I'm on your side." It might have been the only true statement he had ever made to a Toa. He knew the Toa would not believe him, and also knew any efforts by him to claim the mask would serve to reinforce the idea he was just after the artifact. And the Toa would never realize his true purpose . . . not until it was too late.

They probably even think I want them dead, Makuta said to himself. *Another mistake — why should I want their existences to end, when I can look forward to filling them with fear and pain for millennia to come?*

Jaller and Matoro were indeed talking and asking questions during their journey, but not solely about Makuta. After Matoro's confession that he had known all along Makuta was in the body of Maxilos, Jaller had at first been angry. Then, after a while, he realized the impossible spot the Toa of Ice had been in. If Jaller and the other Toa had known, they would have attacked Maxilos. Caught between him and the Barraki, they most likely would have been wiped out and the mission doomed.

"You know, Matoro, you don't have to keep secrets anymore," said the Toa of Fire.

"What?"

"Back when you were a Matoran, working for Turaga Nuju, you heard all sorts of things the Turaga didn't want us to know. Sometimes it seems like they don't want us to know *anything*. You were sworn to keep what you heard to yourself. For years, you knew all about Metru

Nui and what had happened there and you kept it secret."

"I had no choice," said Matoro. "I did what the Turaga felt was best."

"I know that," Jaller said, softening his tone so Matoro would not think he was being attacked. "But doing that made you alone among the rest of us. Now the Mask of Life is doing the same thing and it can't be helped. Still, you have to remember you are part of a team now — you don't have to keep everything inside anymore."

"What do you mean, 'the Mask of Life is doing the same thing'?"

"Do you remember, back on Voya Nui, when Kongu insisted you be the one to take the mask away from Vezon? He didn't explain why at the time. But he told me later that he had read the Ignika's 'mind,' and it wanted you to be the one to carry it. You're the only one who can touch the Mask of Life without being cursed by it. Kongu wasn't sure whether to tell you or not. I told him I would."

Matoro was silent, but his thoughts raced. If he was meant to carry the mask, then did that mean if something happened to him, the mission would fail? And why him? Hahli was faster . . . Hewkii was stronger . . . Jaller and Kongu had way more experience as fighters . . . why would the mask pick him?

"We haven't always been the best of friends," said Jaller. "I guess it's tradition — fire and ice rarely get along. But I wanted you to know . . . I think the Ignika made the right choice."

"You do?" said Matoro, surprised. "Why?"

Jaller smiled. "Because anything you are asked to do — even if it's hard, or painful, or you hate having to do it — you get done. Look, Matoro, back on Voya Nui you once questioned your worth to the team because you aren't a warrior. But being a Toa isn't about who's strongest or toughest or has the best mask power. It's about spirit. And by that measure, you are a great Toa."

Now it was Matoro's turn to smile. Maybe Jaller was right. Maybe he did have what it took to be a Toa. When this mission was over, perhaps he would turn down the chance to become Turaga Matoro and stay a Toa. Even if he couldn't breathe air anymore, there was a whole ocean to explore.

"Thanks, Jaller," said the Toa of Ice. "I mean it."

"No problem," Jaller replied. He chuckled. "Just hang on to that mask, okay? It's been changing hands so fast down here it's made me dizzy."

"Don't worry," said Matoro, looking at the glowing Ignika in his hand. "This time, it's not going anywhere."

"No," said Maxilos. "You're not going anywhere."

He was standing on the ocean floor, confronting the six Barraki. Behind them, their armies could be seen assembling. They were about to launch a final bid to seize the mask, and nothing was going to get in their way — or so they thought, at least.

"Listen to him," snarled Carapar. "Bucket of bolts acting like he's tough. How many pieces should I snap him into?"

"Be careful," said Takadox softly. "He's not what he seems."

"Shut up, Takadox," snapped Kalmah. Mantax had told the others about their fellow Barraki's treachery. They had agreed to let him help get back the mask as a means of atonement for his crimes. But no one doubted he would be dying a painful death before all this was over.

"Carapar, you are an ignorant spawn of a Brakas monkey, and you always were," said Maxilos coolly. "You couldn't snap your fingers without help . . . if you had fingers."

Pridak regarded Maxilos, intrigued. "Takadox is a lying piece of sea slime, but he may be correct in this case. You certainly aren't acting like the robotic guard we knew and loathed all those millennia. But I really don't have the time or interest to ask why. Move aside, or die."

"Do you remember when we first met, Pridak?" asked Maxilos. "Let me see . . . you were standing before me in chains. You talked about how you had once been a servant of the Brotherhood of Makuta, but were moving on to bigger things." Maxilos glanced around at the watery world in which the Barraki dwelled. "When, exactly, are you planning to arrive?"

Pridak, staggered, said nothing at first. Then he was finally able to say the name. "Makuta . . . ?"

The other Barraki stiffened with shock. It had been Makuta who had led the army that shattered their attempt at rebellion 80,000 years before. He was going to execute them, until Botar spirited them away to imprisonment in the Pit. They had nursed an abiding hatred for him and the Brotherhood for all this time.

"It can't be," said Carapar, genuinely confused.

"It obviously is, you dolt," grumbled Kalmah. "What are you doing down here, Makuta? And why the disguise?"

"My reasons for being in this form are my business, not yours," said Maxilos. "As for why I am here — I've come to finish the job I began 80 millennia ago: the destruction of the Barraki."

The six warlords knew they should not waste time on this battle. The Mask of Life was in the hands of the Toa Mahri and they needed to get it back. But . . . the prospect of revenge on the one responsible for their being here was too delicious to pass up. Carapar charged first.

The body of Maxilos never moved so much as an inch as the crab-like Barraki barreled his way. Instead, he called upon one of his many powers to slow Carapar's movement to a crawl. Then he stepped aside and undid his action, allowing the Barraki to resume his all-out attack at the spot where Maxilos once had been. Unable to stop in time, Carapar plowed into a rock wall.

"Hmmm," said Maxilos. "You know, I had forgotten how much fun this is."

"You don't need to tell us," snapped Kalmah, lashing out with his tentacle. "We know all about fighting."

"Fighting? Who's talking about fighting?" replied Maxilos. He unleashed a bolt of chain lightning, stunning all six Barraki at once. "I was talking about winning."

Hahli, Hewkii, Kongu, and Nuparu caught up with their two partners on the outskirts of Mahri Nui. Now that it was abandoned, the village looked like the remains of some long-forgotten shipwreck. Lonely hydruka poked among the fields of air, as if expecting their masters to return at any moment to gather the precious bubbles from the airweed. In a few places around the city, the protective domes of air had weakened to the point that water had flooded in. As the Toa Mahri watched, the largest of the air bubbles collapsed and the sea claimed Mahri Nui.

"Spooky," said Nuparu. "Almost like a giant memorial stone for an entire people."

"Let's hope it doesn't wind up being one for us, too," muttered Kongu.

"The Barraki won't be far behind us," said Hahli. "Whatever we're going to do, we better do quickly."

"Hewkii, you're the one with the dead aim," said Jaller, retrieved Cordah blaster in hand. "What part of the stone cord linking this place to Voya Nui do we target?"

Hewkii's eyes narrowed. Although he no longer wore the Mask of Accuracy he had as a Toa Inika, its power had always been just a supplement to his own natural skill. He was, after all, a former Po-Matoran crafter. He knew all about rock — where it was strongest, where it was weakest, and just how hard to hit to make it split in two.

"There," he said finally, pointing to a narrow spot about 200 yards above the city. "All six of us fire everything we've got at that one point and we'll shatter it. My question is — then what?"

"Axonn said Voya Nui would go back where it came from," said Jaller. "How, I don't know — or how fast. So we better be prepared for anything." He looked around at the rest of the team. "Everyone ready?"

The other Toa Mahri nodded.

"Try hitting the target for a change, Hahli," joked Hewkii.

"Excuse me?" the Toa of Water replied, smiling. "Who won all those kolhii matches?"

"I've never had an island fall-drop on my head before," said Kongu. "This should be interesting."

"New day, new experience," Nuparu said brightly, earning himself a glare from the Toa of Air.

"Um, guys?" said Hahli, pointing behind them. "I just spotted an experience we could do without."

The Toa Mahri turned to see a very angry Gadunka swimming toward them. If the Rahi had suffered any ill effects from his battle with Hewkii, he wasn't showing them.

"It's my old pal," said the Toa of Stone. "Too bad we don't have any of those explosive madu fruit like on our old island. I could teach him to play fetch."

"Your 'pal,' huh?" said Kongu, eyeing the

massive jaws of Gadunka. "Sometimes I wonder about your taste in friends, Hewkii."

"So do I," shot back the Toa of Stone. "Every time I look at you."

"We don't have time for this," said Matoro. "Every minute we waste brings Mata Nui that much closer to dying."

"Don't worry," answered Hewkii. He looked from his weapons to Gadunka, then back to his weapons, and then at Matoro. "Thirty seconds, tops."

That was when the Toa Mahri got their second surprise. Gadunka wasn't alone. Behind him came the 300-foot long venom eel created by the Mask of Life, and the massive sea behemoth summoned from beneath the ocean floor by Kongu's mask during an earlier battle. Initially enemies, the two had apparently made up and befriended Gadunka as well. Now all three had their sights set on Mahri Nui and the Toa.

Hewkii glanced at Matoro. "Better make that forty seconds."

SIX

Maxilos hadn't expected it to be this easy. A mere five minutes into the battle, and already all but two of the Barraki were stretched out unconscious on the sea floor. Either they were not as formidable as he had believed, or else he had simply forgotten just how powerful he could be in battle.

Now only Pridak and Takadox remained. Pridak was battered but still standing, hatred burning in his eyes. Takadox was off cowering somewhere. "Wasn't it enough?" said Pridak, his voice ragged. "You smashed our rebellion all those years ago . . . then stood there as we were dragged off to spend eternity in a cell. Now, when we have another chance at freedom, you stand in our way again! Why?"

"You flatter yourself, Pridak," laughed Maxilos. "Do you think I give a protodite's sigh about you, your ambitions, your freedom? Do you think the leader of the Brotherhood of Makuta traveled all this way simply to stop your freakish band from returning to the land?"

"Then why?" repeated Pridak.

"Because the Mask of Life matters to me," said Maxilos, "and so, by extension, the Toa Mahri matter to me. You, on the other hand, are an inconvenience, like Rahi making noise in the night when your betters wish to slumber. You must be put down."

Takadox suddenly burst out of hiding. In his hand he held the stone tablet of transit. "Makuta! Makuta!" he cried. "Look! See? I hold the Brotherhood of Makuta tablet. This proves I have been loyal! Under Brotherhood law, I must be spared."

Maxilos reached out his hand for the tablet. Takadox dutifully put it in the robot's armored palm. Maxilos regarded it quizzically for a few moments, then glanced up at the eager Takadox. As the Barraki watched, Maxilos closed his fist, crushing the tablet to dust.

"Under Brotherhood law? I *am* Brotherhood law!" said Maxilos. "But since you so obviously want your freedom, Takadox . . . allow me."

Reaching out with his mind, Maxilos enveloped Takadox in his illusion power. Suddenly, the Barraki no longer saw himself as a mutant in the bottom of the watery Pit. Instead, he was in his original form, back on dry land again. He was standing in a castle tower, looking down at his loyal armies. The other five Barraki were there, too, in chains, begging him for mercy.

Any doubts Takadox might have had about this being reality were rapidly dispelled. The sights, the sounds, the smells were so real, down to every detail, how could he help but believe it? Who knew what a Makuta could accomplish, after all?

He gazed out over his realm and his people. All six kingdoms belonged to him now. Oh, he would be a benevolent ruler. He would protect the Matoran in his domain — and they would need protection, since his first act would be the elimination of all Toa within his borders. As for Pridak and the others, he would spare their lives, of course. He would even restore them to positions of importance. After all, the job of keeping the dungeons clean was a vital one in any kingdom.

There was a stirring among the outer ranks of his army. Soldiers were moving aside in a hurry, as if to let someone of importance through. Takadox couldn't see anyone approaching, but the army continued to scatter as whatever it was drew closer and closer to the fortress. Puzzled, Takadox leaned over the parapet to try and catch a glimpse of his visitor. What he saw made him even more confused, and a little worried.

"Why does the ground . . . move?" he said to no one in particular.

Then he saw why. The land before his fortress was covered by a swarm of insects, all headed straight for the walls. But not just one species, no, multiple different kinds of things that crawled and flew and even slithered — and even stranger, all of them were creatures of the sea.

None of the creatures now on the march should have been able to survive more than a few seconds on dry land.

"Oh, no," muttered Takadox. It was his army from the Pit. When he had dwelled below the water, he had commanded legions of undersea insect life. Now he had returned to the land and they had followed. In his heart, he knew they weren't here because they missed him. They were out for revenge.

"Stop them, you idiots!" he yelled at his land-dwelling forces. "What do I pay you for?"

But his army had melted away. The horde of insects had begun to climb the walls now. Takadox turned and flung open the tower door. He was three steps down the staircase before he noticed the stairs were moving as well. That was when he started to scream.

Down in the Pit, Pridak looked with disgust at the screaming Takadox, huddled on the ground with his arms over his head as if to ward off an attack. "What is he seeing?" the Barraki asked Maxilos.

"Something I faced long ago," Maxilos answered. "His destiny. We all have one, you know."

"For good or evil?"

"Nothing quite so antiquated as that," Maxilos chuckled. "For creation or destruction . . . and is creation always good? Is destruction always evil? Suppose I create a weapon capable of ending all life in the universe? Its purpose is destruction, but it was born from creation."

"Yes, I know all about destiny," said Pridak. "Mine was interfered with so you could achieve your ends. It's time I returned the favor."

Maxilos glanced around. Ehlek, Kalmah, Mantax, and Carapar were back on their feet. Their armies had silently assembled all around, with Nocturn swimming at the head of Ehlek's legions. Maxilos was now outnumbered 100,000 to one, at least.

"I see," was all he said. "Your Barraki were not as badly injured as I was led to believe."

"You're not the only talented liar under the sea," said Kalmah. "We were buying time for our armies to arrive. Now we are going to make bait out of you."

Five Barraki and their armies charged, in the greatest attack on a single being in the history of the universe. Maxilos never flinched, never dodged, and never even thought about running as the might of an entire ocean surged toward him. Victory or defeat, he would face his destiny as a Makuta.

The Toa Mahri were in the fight of their lives.

Jaller's battle plan had called for Hewkii to use his Mask of Gravity to take the venom eel out of the fight. But a sudden, violent attack by Gadunka had left the Toa of Stone momentarily stunned. A single blow from the undersea behemoth called forth by Kongu had flattened Jaller and Matoro, and only quick thinking by Nuparu had blocked Gadunka from seizing the Mask of Life.

"You summoned that thing," Hahli said to Kongu. "Can't you make it go away?"

"The mask doesn't work that way," Kongu answered, even as he sent waterspouts slamming into their foes. "But I can summon something else to fight them." Before Hahli could stop him, Kongu called on the power of his Mask of Summoning. He expected some massive pre-historic sea creature to make an appearance for an underwater brawl. Instead, he got a school of tiny, glowing fish, each no bigger than his finger. The Toa of Air looked at them, disap-pointed.

"Stupid mask," he muttered. "What good are they?"

"No, wait, look," Hahli said. The small fish, their natural light flashing on and off, had darted away from the two Toa. As they shot past the whale creature Kongu had summoned before, the beast shot out a slimy appendage and grabbed the entire school. In an instant, it had shoved them into its mouth.

"Well, that's helpful," said Kongu. "I ordered him lunch."

"You did more than that," Hahli replied. "Keep your blaster ready. I have an idea."

The Toa of Water called on the power of her Mask of Kindred, which allowed her to adopt the powers of other sea creatures. This time, she made her body glow with bio-luminescence, as the tiny fish had done. Then she swam toward the whale creature. As soon as it saw her, it thought "meal" and lumbered in pursuit. Hahli dove and dodged as it tried to grab her. Kongu tracked her with his Cordak blaster, waiting for the right moment.

Finally, Hahli darted beneath a huge outcropping of rock, with the massive sea beast following along behind. Just before it passed under the stone formation, Kongu fired his blaster. The projectile struck the rock and exploded, bringing a hail of giant boulders down on the creature. Neither Toa thought it would be enough to kill the beast, but hopefully the avalanche would stun it long enough to take it out of the fight.

Not far away, Hewkii had recovered in time to spot the venom eel bearing down on him, its jaws open wide. A quick use of the Mask of Gravity shut them hard. The Toa of Stone was tempted to use his power to tie the eel into a knot and leave it here, but then he glanced at the cord the Toa were there to destroy. This wasn't going to be the healthiest place to be around pretty soon. It wasn't the eel's fault it was a menace and maybe somewhere else it wouldn't be. And if the Toa Mahri failed in their mission, would any of it matter anyway?

As the eel came around again, Hewkii used his power to lighten its personal gravity just enough to make it unable to fight the current. It was swept rapidly away to the south, struggling in vain to halt its progress. Once outside of the range of the mask's power, it would go back to normal. Hopefully, there would still be a universe for it to live in.

"Okay, forty-five seconds," Hewkii said, as he watched it go.

Elsewhere, Nuparu was having his own problems. He had planted himself between Gadunka and the semi-conscious form of Matoro to stop the creature from getting its claws on the Mask of Life. Using his own mask's stealth power had enabled him to confuse the beast, but Gadunka's eyes rarely strayed from its goal. When Nuparu faded away and then reappeared and his foe took no notice, the Toa knew it was time to try something else.

Nuparu picked up a boulder and threw it with all his strength. Gadunka shrugged and casually bit the rock in half.

Okay. New plan, thought Nuparu.

Unleashing his elemental control over earth, Nuparu ripped a chasm in the ground beneath Gadunka's feet. Startled, the creature tumbled in and was lost from view. Nuparu waited a moment, but there was no further sign of his opponent.

"Glad that's over," Nuparu said, as he turned back to Jaller and Matoro. Both were starting to come around. With all three enemies taken care of, they could get on to their mission here as soon as all six Toa Mahri were assembled.

A pincer tore out of the ground and grabbed Nuparu around the waist. He was lifted off his feet and slammed down on the ground once, twice, three times. Dazed, he turned his head to see he was in the grip of Gadunka. The monster opened its huge jaws and brought Nuparu toward them, intending to make the Toa a meal.

Then something caught the creature's eye. The Mask of Life had flared a little more brightly in Matoro's grasp. Gadunka tossed Nuparu aside, the Toa of Earth already forgotten by its dim brain. Two quick strides took it to its goal. It reached out and grabbed the Mask of Life away from the fallen Matoro.

Had Gadunka's circumstances been different, it might have heard in the past about the unique properties of the Kanohi Ignika. It might have known that those who touch the mask when they are not destined to do so are cursed by it. But Gadunka had not been privileged to have that information, nor would it have known what to do with the knowledge if it had. So it would have to find out the hard way.

The Mask of Life responded with fear and anger to being taken from Matoro. It lashed out, granting Gadunka the power to devolve virtually anything it touched into its original state. The effects were immediate. Before Nuparu's startled eyes, the Rahi began to shrink. As if time had reversed itself, Gadunka rapidly returned to what it had been before the Mask of Life had evolved it mere days ago: a tiny aquatic creature, no threat to anything larger than a darter fish. Deprived of its newfound power and strength, Gadunka roared its frustration — but it was now too small to be heard.

Back on his feet, Matoro went to retrieve the mask. The voice of Hydraxon stopped him. "I wouldn't," said the jailer of the Pit. "That mask comes with me."

Jaller brandished his power sword and Nuparu aimed his blaster at the newcomer. Matoro waved them both off and held the mask out to the battered Hydraxon. "You want this? Take it. Go ahead. Then the fate of the universe can be on your head, instead of mine. I never asked to be the one everything depends upon."

Hydraxon, suspecting a trap, made no move for the mask. "What are you talking about?"

"Use your eyes!" snapped Matoro. "Look around! Strange sea creatures appearing out of nowhere, an entire city of Matoran abandoned, the Barraki and their armies running wild . . . is that normal? And it's probably worse in places like Metru Nui, my home. The end is coming, Hydraxon, even as we stand here talking, and everything that lives can sense it. And now everything comes down to one mask and one Toa — me — and maybe I'm just not up to being a hero. So you take it. You save the universe."

Hydraxon looked at the mask, then into Matoro's eyes. His memories were filled with similar moments, when prisoners had pleaded with or threatened him or insisted on their innocence. No matter what came out of their mouths, their eyes never lied — just as Matoro's were not lying now.

"Maybe I have seen a few strange things," Hydraxon said. He was remembering Maxilos, the things his robot guard had said, and the powers he had displayed. "But that's a pretty powerful mask. What are you planning to do with it?"

Matoro glanced at the glowing Ignika. "When I find out, I'll let you know. So do we have to fight, Hydraxon, or will you let us pass?"

Part of Hydraxon still felt strongly that the Ignika should be destroyed. But a bigger part of him couldn't deny that something felt fundamentally wrong about the universe, even about himself. Maybe these Toa and this mask were the cure for that. If they weren't, there would always be time to bring them in later . . . wouldn't there?

"I have runners to catch," the jailer said. "You can keep your toy for now. But stay out of my way in the future, understand?"

Matoro shook his head. "Somehow, I don't think that will be a problem."

The Toa Mahri stood silently as Hydraxon

swam away. Hahli couldn't help but wonder about the sadness that seemed to hang over the jailer. "It's like he's looking for all these escapees," she remarked, "but he's the one who's really lost."

"Analyze him later. Our troubles aren't over yet," said Hewkii. "Look!"

A wall of darkness was headed straight for the Toa Mahri. It took their eyes a few seconds to process that the "wall" was made up of thousands upon thousands of sea creatures, led by the Barraki. Oddly, Takadox was unconscious and being dragged along by Carapar.

"Well, that's not good," said Hewkii.

"I expected them sooner," said Jaller. "Let's make their trip be for nothing."

All six Toa Mahri wheeled as one, aimed, and unleashed the power of their Cordak blasters. The small projectiles flew rapidly through the water, all of them impacting the same spot on the cord. An instant later, a massive explosion ripped through the stone structure, tearing it in two.

"Move! Move!" Jaller yelled. The other Toa had already gotten the message. All six shot through the water as a great shadow loomed above.

On the surface, the island of Voya Nui shuddered. For centuries, the stone cord and Mahri Nui far below had acted as an anchor, preventing Voya Nui from being drawn back to the continent from which it sprang. Now that anchor had been severed. No power in the known universe could stop Voya Nui now.

The island submerged rapidly, water washing away all the structures built by the Matoran and the Piraka. Voya Nui picked up speed as it dove. Had there been a living being on the island, they would have seen the Toa Mahri, the Barraki, and their legions scattering to get out of the way. About midway to the bottom, the island slowly changed direction, curving in a graceful arc toward the south. The jagged outcroppings on the bottom of Voya Nui struck Mahri Nui as it went by, shattering the undersea island into rubble. Great chunks of stone rained down upon the Pit.

It was one of the most bizarre sights the Toa Mahri could ever remember seeing. A huge island, one they had once walked upon, now rocketing through the water toward an unknown destination as if being pulled on a string. It never slowed — in fact, if anything, it was getting faster — or wavered in its course. It was already halfway across the Pit and would be gone from view in seconds.

The Toa Mahri didn't have time to ponder the insanity of their situation — swimming in pursuit of a runaway island — because they all knew what would happen if they lost this race. Behind them, the enraged Barraki and their legions had recovered from the shock of the explosion and were in pursuit of the Toa.

The last moments of the Great Spirit Mata Nui's life were ticking away. The final countdown had begun.

SEVEN

Matoro swam for his life, and for the lives of every being in the universe.

He clutched the glowing Kanohi Ignika in his hands. It almost seemed like the mask was pulling him along, as if it were being drawn by the same force that was drawing Voya Nui home.

Matoro glanced behind. His fellow Toa were struggling to keep up, but even Hahli was beginning to fall behind after hours of swimming. Coming up fast behind them were the Barraki and their armies, thousands of sea creatures moving like a violent storm through the ocean depths. For just a moment, Matoro's spirit fell — how could six Toa hope to hold off such a mob? And even if they could, would that leave any time to save the life of the Great Spirit Mata Nui?

He pushed those doubts away as best he could. Doubt would be like chains on his feet, slowing his movement and dragging him down. This wasn't the time to question fate — this was the time to face it square, whatever might come.

Up ahead, the land mass of Voya Nui whirled rapidly as it tore through the water, shedding portions of itself as it went. Matoro could only hope Axonn had succeeded in getting all of the Matoran to safety before the stone cord that held Voya Nui in place was destroyed. If not, they were long since dead — *and maybe they will have only beaten the rest of us to it by a few minutes,* he thought grimly.

The mask flared more brightly, illuminating the ocean far ahead. Matoro could dimly make out a massive, ragged hole in the seabed in the distance. Was this where Voya Nui was headed? He knew a huge earthquake more than 1,000 years before had wrenched Voya Nui loose from its continent and sent it shooting upwards through the roof of its underground dome. Could that hole be where it had emerged?

The possibility gave Matoro new energy. He was certain wherever Voya Nui was headed was where the Mask of Life needed to be used. If the Great Spirit could just cling to life for a few moments more . . .

The keen eyes of the Barraki spotted the breach in the ocean floor as well and came to the same conclusion as Matoro. The race was almost at an end.

"Faster!" snarled Pridak. "We have to overtake them! Lose now, and we lose everything!"

Matoro kept on, although his lungs ached and his legs ached and his hands burned where they touched the mask. He had not accomplished a lot in his life prior to becoming a Toa — he had been a watcher, not a doer — but now he had the opportunity to truly matter. He would not go down in history as the Toa who wasn't fast enough, strong enough, or determined enough to save everyone he cared for.

Only a little further, he told himself. *Keep going!*

Voya Nui began to spiral in a downward arc, heading right for the gap in the seabed. The Mask of Life flared brighter than before, almost blinding Matoro with its intense glare. And then . . . it suddenly went dark.

Matoro stopped so abruptly he almost dropped the mask. He felt as if something had been ripped out of his body. Even as a Toa of Ice, he had never truly known what cold was, not until this moment, when all hope was gone.

He knew. How, he couldn't say, but he knew, with the terrible clarity of someone who sees the end coming and cannot move, or scream, or stop the inevitable from happening.

It was over — all of it, over.

The Great Spirit Mata Nui was dead.

Far from the scene, the shattered body of Maxilos dragged itself upright. The Barraki had put up a good fight and it suited him to let them have their moment of victory. The point had been to delay, not destroy them, and if the effort had proved more painful than anticipated, so be it.

Suddenly, the dark presence within the shell of Maxilos felt the universe abruptly shift.

At first, Maxilos could hardly believe it. It had really, truly happened at last. His hated "brother," Mata Nui, had perished! After over 100,000 years of his insufferable concern for the Matoran, his unfailing support of the Toa, and his insistence on light and truth and order, the Great Spirit was no more.

"Mata Nui is dead," he muttered to himself. "Long live Mata Nui."

He could imagine how the Toa Mahri were reacting. Shock . . . disbelief . . . anger . . . maybe even resignation. Time had run out for them and the universe. Toa had been defeated before over the course of history, it was true, but no defeat mattered more than this one. If things stayed as they were, the Mahri would go down in legend as failures — for the few days left in which legends could be created.

But things cannot stay as they are, he said to himself. *The universe, my universe, cannot be allowed to end like this. Mata Nui's weakness will not alter my plans. All of existence ends when I say it ends, not before.*

He was too far away, and his new body too battered, to affect matters directly . . . and there wasn't time. Makuta had no choice but to count on the Toa Mahri to overcome their emotions and press on. Everything depended on them doing what Toa had always done — persisting long past the point any sane being would give up. They *had* to save the life of Mata Nui.

The body of Maxilos shambled away, its occupant voicing a mental wish that the Great Spirit would survive. One might almost call his words a prayer, except that he was praying to himself.

The other Toa Mahri had caught up to the stunned Matoro. They had all felt the abrupt shift in the fabric of existence. Even if they had not, one look at Matoro would have told them what had happened.

The Barraki and their armies were still rushing headlong toward them. Mata Nui's life or death meant nothing to them, if they even sensed it. All they cared about was escape from the Pit, even if there was nowhere left to which they could escape. In a minute, no more, the Toa would be engulfed by the oncoming force.

"We were too late," said Matoro, in shocked tones. "He's dead."

"We will be too, pretty soon," said Hewkii, looking over his shoulder. "The Barraki are desperate. Nothing's going to stop them now."

"Maybe . . . maybe we should destroy the mask," said Kongu. "Make sure it doesn't fall into their hands."

"Even if it did . . . what would it matter now?" said Nuparu.

"No," Matoro said quietly. "No, no, no." He looked at Jaller. "It doesn't end this way. Not without one last try."

"Try? Try what?" said Kongu. "The Great Spirit's dead."

“I don’t know,” said Matoro. “All I do know is that I am holding a Mask of Life. That has to mean something. What if there’s some way to bring him back?”

At one time, Jaller would have dismissed Matoro’s words as insane. But it had not been so very long ago that he had been killed by a Rahkshi then revived through the power of a being called Takanuva. Who could say what was impossible?

“We have to go, now,” said Matoro. “We have to try!”

Jaller looked at Matoro. Then he glanced at the massive armies of the Barraki closing in on them. In the next moment, he left no doubt that he had been destined to be a leader of Toa.

“No,” he said to Matoro. “You have to go. You have to try. The rest of us will stay here and buy you time. Go!”

Toa of Ice looked at Toa of Fire. Traditionally, the avatars of these two elements had clashed, and it had been no different for these two. But Matoro knew what Jaller was saying — he and the other Mahri were prepared to die to give Mata Nui, and Matoro, a chance to live.

It was a moment that called for words . . . and a moment that called for silence. Matoro reached out and shook Jaller's hand, both of them knowing it would be for the last time.

"Make sure to tell the new Chronicler what happened here," said Hewkii. "I'd hate to think we went through all this and don't even get a legend out of it."

"And make sure they pick a good Chronicler," said Hahli, forcing a smile. "Maybe a Ko-Matoran, just to be different."

Too choked with emotion to speak, Matoro turned and started swimming after the island of Voya Nui. Behind him, five Toa Mahri turned to face a wave of evil, prepared to meet their fate.

Exhausted and in pain, Matoro fought to keep moving. Up ahead, Voya Nui had shot down through the hole in the sea floor. The Toa of Ice followed an instant later. The first shock was that there was light down here, provided by scattered lightstones like those used in Metru Nui. The second was that there was another hole far below, one whose shape matched that of Voya Nui perfectly. The gap was in the center of a land mass of enormous size, larger than anything Matoro had ever seen. The third was that this area was not flooded — water was streaming down through the sea floor and down into the second gap, but so vast was the space that even after 1,000 years, it was still mostly dry.

The southern continent, Matoro thought, eyes fixed on the land below. *The Matoran of Voya Nui said their island had once been part of a larger continent before it broke off. And that's where it's returning, but . . . what's that down below?*

The Toa's attention had been drawn to the powerful light coming from the gap in the continent. He had never seen such pure white light before, except when Toa Takanuva was in action. Even though he could tell it was rapidly fading, it was still incredibly bright.

That's where I have to go, he thought, suddenly sure of it. *The light . . . the power . . . the energy . . . that has to be the core of this universe — and where else would the Mask of Life be used?*

Voya Nui was mere moments from slamming back into place. Once it did so, there might be no way to access the core — at least, not quickly enough to do Mata Nui any good. Matoro's only hope was to slip through the gap before the island sealed it off.

He never stopped to consider how he would make his way out once he was inside. All that mattered was saving Mata Nui. There was no room to care about anything beyond that.

Drawing on his very last bit of energy, Matoro raced to outdistance Voya Nui. The island had picked up speed as it got close to home. It was going to be close. If the Toa went fast, but not quite fast enough, he could easily wind up crushed between the island and the continent.

The muscle tissue that held his mechanical parts in place "screamed" in protest as he pushed himself to the breaking point. He was parallel to the island now, falling fast for the gap, and forcing himself to fall faster. Now he was just past it, its giant mass looming over him. The two strange competitors were almost at the gap, but Matoro was still too close to the island.

With one final, desperate burst of speed, the Toa of Ice overtook Voya Nui and shot through the gap. A micro-instant later, the island slammed into the continent, sending a massive tremor through the land mass as it locked into place. Matoro was trapped and in free fall, plummeting down and down through a seemingly endless space.

The Toa Mahri were fighting the good fight . . . and losing.

Spurred on by the maddened Barraki, their sea creature armies were attacking in never-ending waves, heedless of their own safety. The faster the Toa fought them off with weapons and elemental powers, the faster more appeared. The heroes had rapidly become surrounded.

They hovered in the water in a circle, backs to each other, struggling to repel each attack as it came.

Toa Hewkii spotted a school of sharks break off from the rest and head off in pursuit of Matoro. Using his Mask of Gravity, he increased their mass until they slammed into and through the sea floor.

"They're going around us!" shouted Hahli. "We can't stop them all!"

"The Barraki know they just need to tie us down here," Jaller replied, fending off a mob of venom eels. "And if enough of their creatures reach Matoro —"

Hearing the strain in his voice, Hahli glanced over her shoulder at Jaller. The Toa of Fire was glowing white-hot. "What are you doing?" she cried.

"If there's no other chance . . . no other way . . . I am going nova," Jaller answered. "If Matoro is far enough away, and his pursuers still in range . . . well, it may buy him a few more seconds."

"You'll kill us all," said Hewkii. "You know that, right?"

"And all of them," added Kongu. "Plus everything else for kios around."

"If Matoro fails, we're all dead anyway," said Jaller. "But you four can go — try to get out of range — I will wait as long as I can. Don't hesitate — go!"

Hahli shook her head. "We have fought together for over 1,000 years, Jaller. We're not going to stop now. And we'll die together if we have to."

Pridak saw the glow around Jaller and knew instantly what was about to happen. "The Toa of Fire!" he shouted to the other Barraki and their assembled armies. "Destroy him — now!"

In the heart of a waterfall, Matoro fell.

The outside world was a blur of motion. He thought he caught glimpses of high mountains around him. It seemed there was a body of murky water down below, though he could not be sure. At one point, a dark, winged shape flew through the falls just below him, but he could not identify it.

Time was measured in micro-seconds now, flashes of sight and sensation as he plunged deep into the core of the universe. He realized that he had made this leap of faith with absolutely no idea what he was supposed to do with the Mask of Life once he got here. It almost made him laugh. His five best friends were giving their lives for him, and here he was, moments from disaster and still clueless about what it would take to be a hero this day.

Put on the mask.

"What —?" he said, startled. "Who said that?"

There was no answer. Had he really heard that, or was he losing his mind?

Put on the mask.

The Mask of Life — no one really knew the limits of its power. Maybe he was just hallucinating that he heard a voice, but the idea . . . what if the mask had to be, not just carried to the core, but donned for its power to be used? He remembered Takua, the adventurous Matoran who was hailed as the "herald" of a seventh Toa, meant to bring the Mask of Light to him wherever he might be. Little did anyone know Takua was destined to become that Toa, and the hero he had to find was the one who lived inside his own heart.

The universe is a riddle, thought Matoro. *Turaga Nuju often said that. It hints at the path you are meant to walk, but never makes its message clear. You have to figure that out for yourself . . . and maybe I just did.*

With trembling hand, Matoro placed the Kanohi Ignika on top of his own mask. He expected to feel a surge of strength, or perhaps the opposite, a sudden, terrible weakness. But instead he felt . . . different. His body felt light and tingled as if a current of energy ran through it. He was falling still, but no longer tumbling out of control. His form was straight as an arrow and headed for a target still unknown.

Images flashed through Matoro's mind. He saw the creation of the Ignika; its millennia of waiting for the proper time to be used and the destined wearer; he saw it taken from its resting place once before, to be used to heal the Great Spirit . . . and he saw what happened to the one who wore it then.

He didn't cry out, or protest, or rush to tear the mask from his face. Nor did he waste a single moment in regret. He had never asked to become a Toa, or desired it, and the mantle of hero had never fit comfortably on his shoulders. But now, now he knew, and the knowledge brought peace.

Nuju was right. The universe is a riddle. And today, I am the answer.

His arms were thrust out in front of him. They were glowing now, little sparkles of light like the starfield above the island of Mata Nui. His whole body was changing now, patterns of light swirling, energies being unleashed, as the Mask of Life drew forth the essence of the being called Matoro.

Is this the end then? he wondered. *Is this what it feels like?*

Yes, he decided. This was death. This was the price the Ignika demanded for its use. He would no longer exist as Matoro, as a Toa, as a living being of organic muscle and mechanical parts . . . he would be far less than what he was, and far more.

The world was changing all around him, but it did not frighten the Toa of Ice. He knew the real change was in how he was viewing his surroundings — no longer with eyes, a mind, a spirit bound to the physical world. He was becoming pure energy, pure life . . . the force that would bring the Great Spirit back from death. Already, he could barely remember how it felt to be in battle, or to be lonely, or to feel the warmth of a fire on a cold night. Pleasure, pain, satisfaction, disappointment, these were all just words to him now. He was beyond all that, or almost.

But there was one emotion, one part of his former life, that he had not forgotten — one memory he refused to surrender. Jaller, Hahli, Hewkii, Kongu, Nuparu — his friends — his partners — who had fought beside him and laughed with him and made all the burdens bearable. They were out there now in the black water, about to die at the claws of the Barraki. No one on Metru Nui would ever know of their heroism or the sacrifices they were willing to make. They would never see their homes or those they cared about ever again.

His own death, he could accept — but theirs? No, that was too high a price to pay, even to buy the salvation of a universe.

He was Toa Matoro, at least for a few moments more, and he wore the Mask of Life. Or perhaps the Mask of Life now wore him. He didn't know, or care. He knew his friends were willing to die for him and his destiny, and for that reason alone, they had to live.

Matoro pushed back against the power of the mask, fighting to hold on to his consciousness and his own existence for just another heartbeat. He wrestled with the power, pleaded with it, tried to bend it to his will. The Ignika, for reasons of its own, allowed this.

Once before, long ago, a Toa had donned the Ignika and lost his life to complete his mission. That Toa had tried to be brave, but there was fear in his heart and he met his end with grief and regret. The Ignika sensed none of this in Matoro — only a will and determination that rivaled even that of Mata Nui himself.

The Mask of Life, bound now to the energy of Matoro, granted him its power. Matoro seized upon it to perform his final act. It was not one of grand heroism, not a gesture that would shake the universe, but something more powerful and lasting than either one: a simple act of friendship.

With that done, Matoro surrendered himself gratefully and completely to his destiny. The merged energies of Toa and Kanohi mask exploded in the core of the universe, flooding it with light. Streams of golden power flowed into every part of this realm and then beyond it, until it had touched every place where the Great Spirit had once reigned. Just as countless beings had sensed the death of Mata Nui, so did they now feel life return to him. And in the sky above the city of Metru Nui, the stars shone brightly once more. . . .

A few moments ago . . .

Jaller had made his decision. Kongu had already fallen to a treacherous attack by Carapar, and Nuparu had been captured by the forces of Kalmah. Hewkii and Hahli were fighting like wild beasts, but had no chance against the overwhelming numbers of the Barraki forces. There had been no sign of Matoro or that he had succeeded in his mission.

This has to end now, he thought. *I have to make sure that if we're defeated, the Barraki can't stop Matoro or get their hands on the Mask of Life.*

Pridak's efforts to reach Jaller had so far been blocked by the other Toa and by the sheer, overwhelming heat the Toa of Fire was giving off. Now it was time for Jaller to unleash his full power for the first time in one devastating nova burst.

Mata Nui forgive me, he said to himself. He closed his eyes, relaxed his mental control of his fiery energies, and —

"Jaller, stop! Don't! Stop!"

The Toa of Fire opened his eyes abruptly. He saw crystal towers, Ko-Matoran, the familiar sight of the Coliseum — he was back in Metru Nui! With a supreme effort of will, he forced down his nova power before it could devastate his home.

"We're back," he said. "We're back. How is this possible?"

"More than that," said Hewkii. "We're standing on land and breathing air. Thought we couldn't do that?"

Nuparu helped a reviving Kongu to his feet. "Wait a second," said the Toa of Earth. "One of us is missing . . . where's Matoro? If something sent us back here, why didn't it send us all back?"

Then the five Toa Mahri heard a sound they could not recall ever hearing before. It was the voice of Turaga Nuju, speaking Matoran rather than his usual language of clicks and whistles. He was shouting from high atop one of the Knowledge Towers to all of Ko-Metru.

"Mata Nui lives! The Great Spirit lives!"

The Toa Mahri could hardly believe it — Mata Nui had returned to life! They had succeeded! And that meant —

The truth hit them like a blow, driving the smiles from their faces. "Oh, no," whispered Hahli.

"*Something* didn't send us home," said Hewkii. "*Someone* did."

"Matoro," said Jaller. "Then we have to go back. We have to find him. We owe him that."

"We all owe him a great deal more than that." The words came from Turaga Vakama, who was approaching with Nuju. If he seemed surprised by the appearance of the Toa Mahri, he did not show it. "I have seen Matoro's fate . . . felt his thoughts . . . in a vision. There is nothing we can do now but grieve for him."

"I can't . . . believe it," said Hahli.

"He never thought he was a true Toa hero," said Kongu. "He always said he wasn't an athlete or a leader, 'just a translator.' He turned out to be the greatest of us all."

"Come, my friends," said Vakama. "Let us go and celebrate a Ko-Matoran who became a Toa . . . and a Toa who saved a universe."

Turaga Nuju sat alone in the observatory of a Knowledge Tower. All the lightstones in the chamber had been doused. He watched the stars make their flight across the sky in silence. His exultation over Mata Nui's revival had been replaced by grief over the Toa lost in the fight.

Many centuries ago, disaster had forced the Matoran of Metru Nui and their Toa to relocate to a wild, previously unknown island. That disaster had in part been caused by the pride and overconfidence of the Toa, of whom Nuju was one. After the Toa became the village elders called Turaga, they had tried to put the past behind them — all but Nuju. He adopted the language of flying Rahi birds in place of Matoran, only speaking the common language in emergencies. It was his way of reminding the others of what they had been through and the dangers of arrogance.

Of course, speaking another language meant Nuju needed a translator so others could understand him. He chose a Ko-Matoran named Matoro, a hunter/tracker with a real respect for the natural world. Matoro had seemed taken aback by the offer, but eventually agreed to be tutored in Nuju's language.

Over the next 1,000 years, the Turaga and the Matoran would be almost constant companions. Matoro had shown himself to be efficient and trustworthy, keeping all that he heard in the Turaga's councils to himself. Nuju came to rely on him, both for his skills and for his honesty. He was a reminder of the true nobility in every Matoran.

And now he was gone.

The cold, analytical side of Nuju told him this was an acceptable exchange — one Toa for the life of the universe. It was, in fact, a small price to pay for such a monumental event. Feeling regret or sadness was not logical. After all, what was the alternative — Matoro living, and the universe dying? Would that have been better?

For reasons he did not understand and never would, Nuju suddenly realized that the answer might just be yes.

What sort of Great Spirit required the death of a brave, noble hero for his survival? If a being as powerful as Mata Nui could not thrive without demanding such a sacrifice, then maybe existence needed to learn to get along without Mata Nui.

Nuju sighed. No, that wasn't right. If Mata Nui was not worth saving, then Matoro had died for nothing. That he could not accept.

He looked down from the observatory to the streets below. Most of the Matoran residents of the city had not heard about Matoro yet, only that their world was not going to end after all. They were rejoicing. Nuju felt even more detached from them than usual, for in his Knowledge Tower there would be no celebration. There would be only memories of a good translator, an honest Matoran, and — Nuju finally admitted — a lost friend.

EPILOGUE

". . . a Toa who saved a universe."

Hahli stopped speaking. Unsure if she was done, Kopeke waited. It seemed as if she had forgotten he was there. Then a sad smile suddenly flashed across her features.

"I'm sorry, Kopeke," she said. "I was lost in memory. That is all there is to the story. You can carve it on the Wall of History now."

"Is he truly dead?" asked the Chronicler.

Hahli nodded. "He is. But his life force brought Mata Nui back from the endless dark. So you could say that Matoro is a part of everything now — the sky, the waters, the sunlight, and every living thing that walks or flies or swims or crawls. Matoro is dead . . . but never truly gone . . . not as long as the Great Spirit Mata Nui exists."

* * *

In the depths of the Pit, Hydraxon swam alone.

He could not explain all that he had seen in just the last few moments. Mahri Nui destroyed; some other island slicing through the water on its way to who knew where; Toa chasing and being chased; and the Barraki and the armies now turning on each other in frustrated rage.

Nor was that the last of the mysteries. Far below, he saw a gleam of red armor. Nearby, Spinax prowled the sea floor, clawing at the earth as if on the trail of something. Hydraxon dove down to see that the armor did indeed belong to Maxilos. But it was lifeless now. What had happened to the Makuta who had possessed it? Was he dead? Had he simply abandoned the robot body when it became damaged beyond repair? Or was there some other explanation? Hydraxon didn't know.

There was, in truth, a great deal which remained a mystery to him. He would never know that he had once been a Matoran named Dekar before the Mask of Life transformed him, giving him the likeness, powers, and memories of a long-dead hero. He would never realize that his lifelong friends had been safely concealed in the depths of Voya Nui, on their way to begin a new life without him. Perhaps it was best that way . . . ignorance would spare him the pain of brooding on all that he had lost.

Hydraxon gathered up the pieces of Maxilos. He would take the robot somewhere and repair it. And then they would go back to work tracking down runners and bringing them to justice — for there was no other life for either of them.

As he had for so many centuries, Mata Nui slept on.

Turaga and Matoran had wondered for countless ages whether the Great Spirit could sense what was going on in his universe while he slept, or even if he dreamed. Now the answers to these questions could be revealed.

Mata Nui had been aware of the doings in his realm only in bits and pieces over the past millennium. He had sensed his own impending doom, and the absence of the Mask of Life from its accustomed place. In a way he couldn't explain, he knew that Toa had raced to save him from destruction. He felt his own death and his sudden rebirth.

And yes, he dreams now, though he had not done so in the past. Perhaps it is the result of his brush with non-existence, or perhaps something else brought on the images he views. But dream he does — long, torturous nightmares in which darkness claims the world and all who live in it and even the Great Spirit is helpless to prevent it. They are agonizing visions from which he cannot awaken.

And so, one of the most powerful beings in existence can do nothing but hope to someday wake up and find his dreams were only dreams . . . and nothing more.

Tahu, Toa Nuva of Fire, scaled the rocky hillside that led to the fortress of Artakha. Behind him came his five teammates, all strangely silent, as if awed by their surroundings.

It was hard not to feel that way. The island of Artakha was a hidden land whose location had been kept secret for thousands of years. It was said that all those who had any inkling of its location had long ago been hunted down and eliminated. Only after a recent series of quests had the Toa Nuva been given information on how to find the island, and that by a mysterious figure whose face they never saw. He had told them only that they would find something vital to the success of their mission — the awakening of Mata Nui — at the fortress of Artakha.

A long journey over land and sea brought them there. The island had at first seemed lush, tropical and inviting, with happy Matoran hard at work building structures, then taking them apart and rebuilding them. A gleaming fortress stood high atop a grassy hill, the sunlight reflecting off it almost blinding in intensity.

In an instant, everything had changed. The

Matoran dropped their tools and ran for shelters. The sky turned dark and rain fell in sheets. The land transformed from green fields and dense forest to a landscape of twisted, dead plants, rocks, and mud. The fortress shifted as well somehow, becoming a black and forbidding place that would make even a Makuta tremble.

"Gali, Lewa, can you do something about this storm?" Tahu yelled, trying to make himself heard above the wind.

The Toa Nuva of Water and Air both nodded. Combining their powers, they attempted to dispel the raging thunderstorm overhead. After a few moments, they gave up, defeated.

"Whatever is causing this is greater than our powers can deal with," Gali said. "Do you think this is the work of Artakha himself?"

"If it is, he and I are going to have a long deep-talk," said Lewa. "Fine way to treat guests."

They had reached the massive iron doors of the fortress. There was no sign of a knocker or any other way to signal their presence. As it turned out, none was needed.

"Who are you? Why have you come here?"

The voice was indescribably ancient, and yet young at the same time. It came from everywhere around them — the fortress, the rocks, the trees, even the air itself.

Tahu took a deep breath. This had to be Artakha talking to them. It wasn't easy to know how to answer a legend. Artakha was rumored to be the greatest builder and designer in the universe. Some of the greatest artifacts known, from the Mask of Light to the Mask of Shadows to the Nuva masks he and his friends wore, were said to have come from Artakha's forge. Yet, if the stories were to be believed, no one had actually seen Artakha in all the millennia of his existence.

Maybe that is about to change, thought Tahu.

"We are —" he began, then stopped. "But you already know, don't you?"

"Does the sun know its light?" the voice responded. "You have come here to find arms and armor for your fight. I tell you that the weapon you need cannot be found here — that must be sought in the world that feeds the world. As for the other . . ."

The storm suddenly abated as quickly as it had arisen, replaced by a cold wind that made even the Toa Nuva of Ice shiver. Sleet and snow began to fall, half burying the Toa in a matter of moments.

"Tell me what you have done on your path to this place," said the voice of Artakha.

"Are we here to play games?" Kopaka Nuva responded. "Your name is spoken with respect in a thousand places, Artakha. I begin to wonder if those who honor you have been deceived."

Artakha's laughter was like thunderclaps. "You amuse a being who was already weary of life when you first set foot on solid ground, Toa. And there is iron behind your icy facade — that is good. You were made far better than anyone knew. But my question still needs answering."

Tahu swiftly described the Toa Nuva's most recent adventures, including the freeing of the imprisoned Bahrag, the downfall of the realm of

Karzahni, and the assault on the island of the Dark Hunters. Artakha said nothing, merely listened.

When Tahu was finished, there was a long period of silence. Then the snow and sleet were gone, replaced by warmth and sunlight. When the ice melted away from the Toa, it left behind gleaming masks and armor on the ground at their feet.

"You have done all that has been asked of you, and more," said Artakha. "You have earned these masks and armor. Wear them well, for they are perhaps my greatest creation. Wherever you journey, they will adapt to your surroundings. No terrain, no climate, no wind or wave will ever again be your master.

"Now you must leave here. The time has come at last for the Great Spirit Mata Nui to awaken — and you must be the ones to bring him back to those who need him."

"Wait!" said Tahu Nuva. "Let us see you!"

"Come with us!" said Onua Nuva, Toa of Earth. "Your aid would be welcome, Artakha."

"No," said Artakha, even as the Toa Nuva's vision began to blur. "Where you travel, you must travel alone."

A moment later, the island of Artakha was gone — or so it seemed. In fact, the Toa Nuva had been transported from the island by the power of its ruler. When their vision finally cleared, they were in mid-air, high above a strange Matoran village. Somehow, their armor had shifted in a hundred ways, making it possible for them to stay aloft. But there was no time to wonder about that — all around them, a battle raged in the sky.

"Go, Toa Nuva," the voice of Artakha echoed throughout this new land. "Go and find your destiny at last!"

END